THE LIE SHE PROMISED

A Novel by Isla March

*"Some truths kill you slowly.
Others just wait until you beg for them."*

**Royston Knight
Publishing**

TRUTH. WIT. INK.

CONTENTS

Foreword

I was not always the woman who stood at the window watching the sea, hoping it would rise and take the house. Once, I believed in memory — not as truth, but as something gentler, like a song you half-remember in the dark.
Now I know better.

We don't remember what happened.
We remember what we were told.
And sometimes, we remember what we needed to believe in order to survive.

This is not a confession.
This is a reconstruction.
Of what was said. Of what was left unsaid. Of what she promised me —
and what I promised her, when I thought she might still be real.

If you are reading this, then you already know something went wrong.

The First Knock

The Envelope Wasn't Addressed to Me

The sound was so gentle I thought it was the wind at first — a dull tap against the old brass letterbox. It hadn't made a sound in months; all my post came digitally now, or not at all. No one wrote to me anymore. No one should've known where I lived.

I was halfway through washing the breakfast cup — porcelain, hairline crack through the handle — when it came again. A second knock, soft but deliberate. Like someone was testing the memory of the house. Or of me.

I dried my hands on the hem of my jumper and opened the door.

Nothing.

Only a thick white envelope resting on the stone doorstep, the kind you used to get exam results in. No address. No stamp. Just my name, in handwriting so careful it might have been forged.

Eve Whitaker.

Not Dr. Whitaker. Not Ms. Nothing. Just Eve. Like they knew me before.

I didn't open it right away.

Instead, I sat back at the kitchen table, the envelope on the placemat beside the cup I hadn't yet refilled. I told myself I was being ridiculous — people send things, even in small towns like this. Perhaps it was from the council. Or the woman from the book club I'd quit after three sessions. Perhaps it was harmless.

But it didn't feel harmless.

There was something about the weight of it — not heavy, but intentional. Like it contained a truth I'd forgotten how to carry.

My fingers found the edge of the flap almost without thinking. A soft tear, a whisper of glue unsticking from paper. Then the note.

Just one sheet. Folded once.

Typed.

> *"You saw what she did. You just didn't want to believe it."*
> *— A Friend*

I didn't drop it. I didn't gasp. I didn't even blink.

But something inside me — something old and partially cauterised — shifted. Like a healed bone cracking open on a cold morning. Like a ghost remembering the route back to its house.

I read the note again.

You saw what she did.

My first thought wasn't *Who?*

It was *How did they know I did nothing?*

Things That Should Have Stayed Buried

I told myself not to pace, but I did. From the kitchen to the hallway and back again, trailing invisible footprints into the same groove I always slipped into when memory refused to stay where I'd left it. Outside, the sea was flat and stubborn, grey as old milk. A coastal lull — the kind that made you feel watched, even when you knew better.

I didn't keep the note in the bin. That would've been too easy.

I burned it.

In the ceramic ashtray I never used. Watched the edges curl in on themselves, like a secret recoiling from the light. The final word to disappear was *Friend*.

And that unsettled me more than the accusation.

I tried to return to the day as if nothing had happened. Made the bed. Rearranged the bookshelf. Answered an email from someone trying to sell me grief counselling, which felt cruelly ironic. I even peeled an apple and sliced it into fan shapes, the way I used to do when I was seeing clients — little things that made you look like a functioning human.

But I couldn't stop thinking about her. About Marianne.

The woman who once told me that trust was just love with a deadline.

The woman who'd rewritten my beliefs one late-night session at a time until I couldn't tell where hers ended and mine began.

The woman who had taught me to unravel people gently, like silk.

And the woman I hadn't seen in eight years — not since the morning after everything came undone.

It wasn't just the content of the note. It was the precision of the words. The calmness. Whoever wrote it hadn't intended to frighten me.

They intended to make me doubt myself again.

It worked.

I stood in front of the mirror above the hallway radiator and tried to see what they might see. A woman who'd rebuilt her life with deliberate symmetry. The minimalist flat, the quiet job cataloguing psychological case studies for a publishing house that never asked too many questions, the quiet seaside postcode.

I was no longer a therapist. No longer anyone's confessor, saviour, or scapegoat. I'd erased that version of me with the kind of control only a former insider could manage. I knew the rules — burn the credentials, change the contact details, never Google her name.

And yet.

The note sat in the space between my ribs, where panic used to live.

There had been signs, of course. Little things that I'd filed under *unsettling but explainable.*

The blurred-out photograph that someone emailed me last winter with no subject line — just a grainy still of a hallway I recognised from Marianne's old clinic.

The review left on an obscure psychology blog: *"Even the brightest minds cast shadows when they refuse to look back."* It had been deleted within hours, but I'd seen it.

And now this note.

Someone was building a breadcrumb trail. But to what? The truth about her?

Or the truth about me?

I sat down with my journal — a habit I'd dropped but still reached for in moments like this. I didn't write what I felt. I wrote what I remembered. Which is not the same thing.

> *She was charismatic.*
> *She knew how to enter a room without seeming to.*
> *She told me things I hadn't told myself yet.*
> *She taught me how to listen for what people were hiding.*
> *She never raised her voice, but she always made me feel loud.*

I stopped, pen hovering over the paper.

She made me lie for her.

I crossed the sentence out, but the indentation on the page remained.

The Patient She Shouldn't Have Taken

The first time I met Marianne Vale, she wasn't *my* supervisor. She wasn't even introduced to me. She was just there — watching from the end of the corridor like a woman waiting for her cue.

It was my second week of clinical placement, and I was already losing sleep over how quickly we were expected to make sense of other people's pain. They taught us the ethical frameworks, the DSM criteria, the vocabulary of treatment. But they didn't teach us what to do when someone walked in bleeding the kind of grief that couldn't be quantified. They didn't tell us how to sit in a room and not absorb someone else's ruin.

Marianne knew, though.

She walked into my tutorial that day and said, "You'll only be useful to your clients when you've stopped trying to rescue them."

I remember the way the other students sat up straighter when she entered. I didn't. I just watched her. She wasn't beautiful in the ordinary sense, but she was magnetic — too still for someone alive. Her eyes didn't blink as often as they should. And when she looked at me, it was like she'd already decided I belonged to her.

She chose me.

There's no other way to put it. I didn't ask her to mentor me. I didn't even think I was ready for that kind of attention. But she saw something — some crack, some softness, some unhealed thing I wore like perfume — and she pressed into it gently. She made space for me. She told me I had "emotional clarity". She said I reminded her of herself before she learned restraint.

And so I became her shadow.

The kind of eager, grateful student who clung to every insight like it was gospel. I didn't realise until years later that most of what she taught me was designed to make me complicit.

The patient in question came during our third year of supervision.

A girl, nineteen, fragile in the way that made you lean in instead of away. Her name was Lily, though she sometimes forgot it. Trauma-induced dissociation. Long-term abuse. A mother who alternated between neglect and religion. Lily had come to us after a suicide attempt. She'd been assigned to me — but Marianne overrode the placement.

"She needs a tighter container," she said. "She needs me."

I didn't object. How could I? Marianne had a way of making you believe that her choices were not just correct, but inevitable.

But over the weeks, I began to notice things.

Marianne's sessions with Lily often ran long. She cancelled other clients to make time for her. She never wrote up notes — a red flag in any clinical setting. And Lily's attachment to her became something heavy. Worshipful.

"I think she's scared of losing you," I said once, in supervision.

Marianne only smiled. "That's how we know we're getting somewhere."

I should have said something.

But I didn't. Because I trusted her. Because I wanted her approval. Because I had come to believe that she *couldn't* be wrong — that everything she did had a higher psychological purpose. Even when it felt off. Even when Lily started talking about dying again.

"She says she'll do it if you stop seeing her," I told Marianne.

"She won't," she replied, calmly. "She's trying to test the limits of containment. If we panic, she wins."

That phrase has stayed with me.

If we panic, she wins.

It turned Lily into an opponent, not a patient. A manipulator, not a survivor.

And a week later, Lily was dead.

They ruled it suicide. She'd left a note, though its contents were never made public. I never saw it. But something in Marianne shifted after that.

Not grief. Not guilt.

Just a tightening. A new version of her emerged — colder, more precise, less human. And I watched it happen without stopping it.

Because if I'd intervened, I'd have to admit that I'd known.

That I'd seen the lines blur, and said nothing.

And now, someone else knew I had.

The Return of Her Voice

That night, I dreamed in fragments. Not full scenes, but splinters. Her voice. The sound of Lily's laugh. A white room with no windows. Marianne's hands — always manicured, always composed — holding a box I couldn't open. When I woke, the sheets were twisted around my legs like vines.

It was 4:43 a.m.

I didn't reach for my phone. I sat up slowly and stared into the dark, listening. As if the walls might speak. As if the sea might whisper its own warning.

They say the body remembers before the mind does. Mine did. The weight in my chest wasn't panic — it was prelude.

I should have gone back to sleep.

Instead, I went to the study.

There was a locked drawer in the bottom of the desk — one I hadn't opened in three years. Not since I moved here and decided to keep my past in paperwork rather than memory. The key was taped to the back of a photograph in the frame on the windowsill. A smiling version of me beside a lake, half-blinded by the sun. Someone else's idea of who I used to be.

The lock clicked open.

Inside: old files. Clinical notes I'd never submitted. Personal journal pages torn out in fury. Newspaper clippings about Lily's death. All things I'd sworn I didn't keep.

And at the very bottom — a memory stick. Black, unlabeled, easily missable.

My breath caught.

I hadn't seen it in years. Had nearly convinced myself it didn't exist.

The file was dated exactly one week before Lily's death. A voice recording. Marianne's voice.

I hesitated before pressing play, irrationally certain she'd somehow know I was listening.

Then:

> "It's not about what happened to you, Lily. It's about who you've become because of it."

Pause.

> "You can't keep using your past as permission to fall apart. At some point, the story has to change. Or you die in the same chapter."

My skin prickled.

Another pause. A breath — not Marianne's. Lily's.

Then a soft, broken whisper.

"But I don't know who I'd be without the pain."

Marianne's reply was chilling in its composure.

"Then maybe it's time to let the pain go. One way or another."

The file ended there.

I closed the laptop.

I had never heard that recording before. I hadn't even known it existed — or had blocked it out.

Had Marianne known it was on my drive?

Had I recorded it myself during supervision and forgotten?

Or had Lily sent it to me, and I'd buried the memory along with the evidence?

Either way, it was damning. Not legally — not directly. But in the soft spaces. In the nuance. In the silence between Marianne's sentences, where Lily's desperation sat, ignored.

I should have done something then.

But instead, I poured a glass of water and sat in the dark, wondering how many truths I had kept just to keep functioning.

And who, exactly, had just reminded me of them.

The next morning, I received a text from an unknown number.

"We should talk. There's more."

No name.

No context.

But I knew. Deep in the hollow of my gut, I knew.

She was back.

And this time, she wasn't hiding.

A Face I Never Expected to See Again

I didn't respond to the message. Not immediately. Not with words, at least.

Instead, I drove.

An old impulse, automatic as breath. Whenever something rose too quickly — memories, panic, grief — I drove until my nerves stopped vibrating. Through back lanes, down roads I hadn't named aloud in years, the past thickening with every mile.

It had rained in the night. Everything was slick with leftover storm — puddles collecting secrets, trees trembling, sky still low and brimming.

I had no destination. Only a direction: inland. Away from the coast, away from the little house that had pretended to be a safe place. I passed signs for places I hadn't allowed myself to revisit.

And then, just after noon, I turned into a layby outside a small café with peeling green shutters. Familiar. Unchanged.

And parked there, already waiting, was the only face I never thought I'd see again.

Marianne Vale looked different.

Not in the dramatic way — no new face, no dye job, no reinvention to escape recognition. She had always been cleverer than that. But the years had smoothed her, refined her. She looked expensive in a way that whispered, not shouted. Cashmere scarf. Minimal makeup. The kind of understated polish that makes people lean in, not recoil.

And her expression — it was exactly as I remembered. Kind. Controlled. Vaguely maternal.

Which made me want to scream.

She stood as I approached, opening her arms like an old friend welcoming a reunion.

"Eve," she said softly, like it was still her right to say my name.

I didn't hug her. I didn't even touch her.

I just said: "Why now?"

We sat at a table by the window, the kind that still bore the faint carvings of teenage initials from decades past. She ordered Earl Grey. I asked for nothing. I didn't trust my hands not to shake.

She looked at me like I was still hers — something precious she'd lost in a fire.

"I've missed you," she said.

"You always did open with a lie."

She didn't flinch. "You haven't lost your sharpness."

I leaned forward. "Who sent the note?"

A pause. A flicker.

"I don't know."

I laughed. It wasn't funny, but my body needed the noise.

"Don't insult me, Marianne."

Her eyes softened, as if she was sorry I still needed things like truth.

"I didn't come to hurt you, Eve."

"Then why *did* you come?"

She sipped her tea, as though the answer needed steeping.

"There's been… some attention. An inquiry. Informal, but persistent. Someone's asking questions. About Lily. About my former clients. And about you."

"Why me?"

"Because you were closest to her. Because you kept records you shouldn't have. Because…" She trailed off, then added gently, "Because they know you were the last person she tried to contact."

That stopped me.

She must've seen the shift in my posture, because she placed her cup down very deliberately.

"I came to warn you," she said.

"I don't need your warnings."

"You do. You just don't want to hear them from me."

She reached into her bag and slid something across the table — an envelope. This time addressed. My old name. My former address in London. Postmarked only three weeks ago.

"Where did you get this?" I asked.

"It was intercepted. I still have contacts in places that matter."

I opened it, heart pounding.

Inside: a photocopy of a page from Lily's patient notes — the real ones. With a line I recognised instantly.

> *'If something happens to me, ask Eve. She knows the truth.'*

I didn't speak. Couldn't.

Marianne said nothing for a long time. Just sat there, watching me absorb it. Watching me break.

Then, finally, she leaned in and said quietly:

"Someone wants to exhume the story we buried. And they're not going to stop at shadows."

The Second Letter Arrives

I didn't go straight home.

After Marianne left — with her cryptic warnings and her tragic eyes and that voice still polished enough to pass for care — I sat in the car for almost an hour. Engine off. Hands still on the wheel. Staring at the ghost of my reflection in the windscreen, trying to decide whether I was more frightened of the truth coming back, or the possibility that it never really left.

The envelope still sat in my coat pocket, the one she'd slid across the table with surgical calm. I could feel it pressing into my ribs as I drove. A reminder, a bruise. Something Lily had written — or been coaxed to write — preserved long after her death.

Ask Eve. She knows the truth.

I don't remember driving back. Only the sea, flat again. The stillness you get before something breaks.

The house was cold when I entered. I didn't notice at first. I didn't notice anything, not until I reached the kitchen and found another envelope waiting for me.

No knock this time. No warning. Just there, like it had grown up through the tiles while I was gone.

This one was different.

Typed. Larger. And sealed with a single strip of masking tape.

My full name again. But this time, the old one:
Dr Eve Whitaker
Not just Eve.

A correction.

Or a challenge.

I didn't open it straight away.

I made tea first. Stood at the counter and watched the kettle hiss like it was trying to warn me. My hands were steady now — oddly so. I'd slipped past the panic and into the hollow place beyond it.

Only when the water had cooled slightly did I slide my finger beneath the tape.

Inside, no note this time.

Just a photograph.

A printed one — glossy, high-res, too modern to feel safely distant. It showed the back of a building I recognised instantly. A clinic, once private, now defunct. Burnt out at the edges. Shuttered after the incident that never made the headlines.

Marianne's former practice.

But that wasn't the part that stopped my breath.

In the corner of the photo — barely visible unless you knew where to look — was a face behind a window.

Mine.

It took me a moment to accept it.

My hair was different then — darker, shorter — but it was me. Watching from the second floor, where the one-way mirrors were used during assessments. I looked younger. More hopeful. And frightened.

This photo had been taken at least nine years ago.

Someone had kept it. Stored it. Waited for the right moment to send it.

And now they wanted me to know: *I see you. I remember.*

I sat down, photo in hand, and began piecing the timeline.

Lily died in March. The clinic shut down that summer. Marianne disappeared two weeks later. I stayed — for a while — trying to finish my training in a hospital setting. I was never officially investigated. No one ever said anything outright.

But I remember the way they stopped asking for my opinion in rounds.

I remember the day they took my ID badge early — "just a formality."

And I remember, vividly, the last voicemail Marianne ever left me:

> *"It's better to let them believe what they want. Don't defend me, Eve. It makes you look guilty."*

I never deleted it. Just buried it under a thousand others. Until now.

Whoever was behind the notes — the photograph — the warnings — they weren't just dredging up Lily's death.

They were excavating *me*.

Piece by piece.

And for the first time in years, I found myself wondering what they were hoping to prove.

That Marianne was dangerous?

Or that I was complicit?

Either way, someone had appointed themselves archivist of a story I no longer wanted to tell.

And this time, I didn't know where it would end.

The Rehearsal of Guilt

There are things I used to say to patients when they were caught between memory and shame. Phrases I'd polished, professionalised — bite-sized insights dressed up as kindness.

"You're not what happened to you."
"Guilt is just grief with a direction."
"Sometimes survival looks like silence."

I said them because they worked. Or at least, they sounded like they did.

But when I stood in the mirror that night, trying to rehearse my face for the version of events I might need to defend one day, none of them fit anymore.

Because guilt wasn't just grief.

Guilt was knowing I *had* been warned — and had chosen the woman over the girl.

I hadn't seen Lily cry until her final month of sessions. Before that, she'd been all flint and performance, like she knew she was being watched. She often was — that clinic had mirrors in too many places, and Marianne believed in observation like a religion.

But that day, something slipped.

I was on admin duty, filling out referral reports, when I passed Lily in the corridor. She didn't see me at first. She was on the bench near Marianne's office, her knees drawn up under her hoodie, face hidden in the crook of her elbow.

Then the sob — raw, sudden. A sound like something had broken just then, on the spot.

I paused.

I shouldn't have.

We weren't supposed to interfere with one another's clients — a rule drilled into us from week one. It muddied the therapeutic relationship. Undermined trust. But that sob didn't sound like something that belonged in paperwork.

I stepped forward.

"Lily?"

She looked up — startled, then soft. Her face was blotched, her eyes dark-rimmed with salt and mascara. Not the performance this time.

And in that moment, she said something I've never forgotten.

> "She says I make it up. That I romanticise the pain."

I crouched beside her, the air too still.

"Who says that?"

"You know who." A bitter smile. "Your mentor. She says the trauma's my identity. That I'd fall apart without it."

I tried to find a response. Something professional. Something careful.

But she went on.

"Do you think she's right?"

I didn't answer.

I didn't get the chance.

Marianne opened her office door just then, and the energy in the corridor shifted like a fault line cracking open. Lily stood abruptly, wiping her face, already tucking the emotion away.

And Marianne smiled like she hadn't just heard everything.

"Ready, darling?"

Her voice was warm. Too warm.

Lily nodded. Then glanced back at me, just once, as if daring me to follow.

But I didn't.

I stayed frozen. A bystander in my own memory.

That was the moment. I know that now. The one where everything might have changed.

That's the problem with guilt.

It doesn't scream. It settles.

It curls up in the corners of your mind and hums while you try to sleep. It feeds on what-ifs and might-have-beens.

And sometimes it dresses itself up as justice — like when I found myself scrolling through Marianne's old articles that night, searching for proof I hadn't imagined it all.

She still had a presence online. Carefully curated. A podcast episode here, a glowing quote there. No mention of Lily. No shadows in the spotlight.

She'd reinvented herself as a specialist in *post-traumatic reprogramming* — whatever that meant. A way of reframing pain so it no longer held power. She even had a book coming out.

The Promise of Rewriting: Trauma as Narrative Choice.

I read the blurb twice. Once in disbelief, and once in quiet fury.

Because that was her gift — taking someone's suffering and branding it with her own name.

My phone buzzed.

A new message. Same unknown number.

"Do you remember what she said the last day you saw her?"

I didn't reply.

But the truth was:
Yes.
I remembered every word.
And I'd never said them aloud.

The Words She Left Me

It was raining the last time I saw Lily alive. Not symbolic rain — not the kind you write about to suggest grief or foreshadowing. Just a persistent, grey drizzle that soaked into clothes and made people meaner to one another in shop queues.

She was scheduled for a morning session with Marianne. I wasn't on rotation that day, but I'd come in anyway — some leftover obligation pulling me back. The building smelled of old paint and wet carpet. The kind of place that had seen too many stories and carried all of them badly.

Lily arrived late. I remember the receptionist whispering something about traffic, but when she walked in, her eyes were bloodshot and her coat was buttoned wrong. She looked both older and younger than nineteen, like she'd fast-forwarded through years in one night and hadn't caught up.

I caught her eye as she passed. She paused.

Just for a second.

Then she said it.

> "If I don't come out, will you still pretend you didn't know?"

She said it like a dare. But there was no venom in her voice. Just exhaustion. The kind you only hear when someone's already gone in their mind.

And then she disappeared down the corridor.

I didn't follow.

I didn't check in.

I didn't knock on Marianne's door, even when my skin prickled with something that wasn't quite dread but wasn't far off.

I sat at the desk and typed reports. I signed off on emails. I existed beside something monstrous and told myself I was powerless.

Three days later, Lily's body was found in her flat. The official line was that she'd taken a mix of prescription medication and alcohol. No evidence of external injury. No suggestion of foul play.

Just a quiet end. Unremarkable on paper.

But I remembered her words.

Will you still pretend you didn't know?

It was only after she died that I read the transcripts.

Not therapy notes — those were sealed. But I had access, briefly, to an audio extract Marianne had sent in as part of a conference paper, back when she was being celebrated for her innovative trauma techniques.

It wasn't marked as Lily's file, but I knew her voice.

She was speaking softly, hesitantly.

> "I feel like I'm standing on the edge of something sharp. And everyone keeps telling me to look at the view instead."

Then silence.

Then Marianne's voice — cool, calm, surgical.

> "It's time you understood the difference between drama and suffering, Lily. One gets you attention. The other gets you nowhere."

I'd closed the file after that.

And I'd never reopened it.

Now, sitting in my kitchen again, with the weight of memory thick in my throat and a stranger texting me fragments of my own past, I finally understood something.

They weren't trying to frighten me.

They were trying to *remind* me.

Of the cost of complicity.

Of the silence I'd chosen.

Of the girl who asked me to witness her, and the woman who taught me to look away.

I opened my journal. Wrote a single line.

"If I am called to testify, I will not protect her."

Then I tore the page out.

Burned it.

Because I still wasn't ready to keep a promise — even to myself.

The doorbell rang.

This time, it wasn't an envelope.

It was a person.

And she knew my name.

The Stranger at My Door

She looked about twenty-three, maybe twenty-four. Young enough to carry hope in her bones but with a gaze that had already rehearsed disappointment. Her hair was tied up in a way that looked accidental, like she'd run out of time, or maybe just didn't believe she was worth the mirror.

She didn't introduce herself at first. Just stood on the threshold in a denim jacket far too thin for the weather, clutching a manila folder like it might fly away if she let go.

"I'm sorry," she said. "I know you weren't expecting anyone."

Her voice was quiet. Almost cautious.

Something about her posture — the way she tilted slightly forward, like she wanted to be let in but wouldn't ask — undid me.

I didn't ask how she knew where I lived.

I didn't ask who sent her.

I just stepped back and let her inside.

She sat at the kitchen table, hands curled around a mug she didn't drink from.

"I'm not here to cause trouble," she said. "I just... I thought you should see this."

She opened the folder and slid it across the table.

Inside: newspaper cuttings, mostly old. One I recognised instantly — *YOUNG WOMAN FOUND DEAD AFTER MENTAL HEALTH STRUGGLES* — Lily's death, reduced to four paragraphs and a blurry stock photo. Others I didn't recognise. But the pattern emerged quickly.

All female. All under thirty. All clients of now-defunct therapy clinics.

All suicides.

My stomach turned cold.

"These weren't connected," I said, more to myself than to her.

"No," she said. "But they should have been."

Her name was **Georgia**.

She wasn't a journalist, or a whistleblower. She didn't work in mental health.

She was Lily's half-sister.

Same father, different mothers. They hadn't grown up together — in fact, Lily hadn't even known about her until just before she died. Georgia had reached out, a tentative message through social media, a few exchanged texts. Nothing dramatic. Nothing intimate.

But it was enough to make Lily feel like she might not be entirely alone.

Then, silence.

And then the obituary.

"I didn't believe it," Georgia said. "Not the way they told it. So I started digging."

She'd traced Lily's therapy history. Found Marianne's name. Found mine.

"I wanted to hate you," she said, staring at the table. "I thought maybe you'd been the one to push her. But the more I read, the more I think you were… trapped."

I didn't answer.

Because I wasn't ready for forgiveness from someone I hadn't even met.

Georgia pulled out a second envelope.

"This came to me three months ago," she said. "No return address. Just… this."

Inside was a printout of a scanned journal entry. It was dated the week before Lily's death.

The handwriting was hers.

I'd seen it often enough on intake forms and therapy worksheets — rounded, looping, always tentative.

If I don't make it, it wasn't because I was broken.

It was because someone decided I was too difficult to fix.

Someone who knew better. Someone I trusted.

She hadn't named names.

But she didn't need to.

Georgia's voice cracked slightly.

"I think someone sent it to me so I'd keep going. So I wouldn't let it die quietly."

I nodded.

"Do you think it was her?" she asked.

"Marianne?"

"No. Lily. Do you think she planned this? Left pieces behind?"

I paused.

Then: "I think she knew how easily people forget the girls who don't fit into survivor stories."

The room was silent for a long time.

Outside, the sea whispered something cruel against the windows.

Then Georgia looked up.

"She's trying to disappear again, isn't she?"

I nodded once.

"But this time," I said, "someone's watching."

The Revival of the Case No One Wanted

Georgia left just after dusk, the folder under her arm and the mug of untouched tea still warm on the table.

She hadn't asked for anything. Not answers. Not alliance. Not absolution. Just confirmation that she wasn't going mad for noticing what the professionals had ignored — or perhaps buried.

She said she'd be in touch. That there were more threads to follow. That if she found something, she'd share it.

But I already knew what she would find.

Because I'd lived it.

And I'd spent years telling myself it wasn't my story to tell.

I watched her from the window as she disappeared down the lane, small against the night. And then, when I was sure she was gone, I unlocked the cupboard I hadn't opened since moving into the house. Not even once.

Inside, beneath old books and outdated journals, was a cardboard box. Unlabelled. Taped shut.

Inside that: five case files.

Not copies.

Originals.

Each one signed in Marianne's unmistakable cursive. Each one stamped and dated from the clinic's final year.

Each one redacted in sections that I had restored.

I'd told myself I kept them to protect myself — insurance, in case Marianne ever came after me. But that wasn't the truth.

I'd kept them because I couldn't bear the idea that no one would ever know what really happened to those girls.

What was done to them under the guise of treatment.

What wasn't done — the support withheld, the manipulation disguised as mentorship, the love offered as bait.

Each file told a version of the same story.

Young woman, high risk, charismatic but emotionally volatile.

Each one had shown signs of trauma bonding — first to Marianne, then to the therapy space itself.

Each one had either left abruptly, suffered a breakdown, or in Lily's case… disappeared altogether.

But the language in the notes — the way Marianne had written them — it was meticulous. Clinical. She used phrases like *emotional dependency*, *fabricated narratives*, *secondary gain*. Words that turned survival mechanisms into pathology.

I knew the tone well.

I had once admired it.

Now it felt like a scalpel.

But the fifth file was the one I hadn't let myself read until now.

Because it was the one I had written.

E. Whitaker
Supervised case notes
Subject: "L"

The first page was blank.

Then a single sentence, in my own handwriting:

> *I'm still not sure who I was protecting — her,*
> *or me.*

My phone buzzed again.

Georgia, this time.

A link.

No text.

It led to an anonymous blog post on a survivor's forum — not public, but shared among a small, closed network.

The title was simple.

"She Told Me I Was Imagining the Hurt."

I scrolled.

Paragraph after paragraph of a familiar voice. Not Lily's — someone else. A different girl. A different time.

But the shape of the pain was the same.

She had been in therapy with *M. Vale*. She had left, disoriented and ashamed. She had questioned her own memories. She had almost given up.

But now, she was speaking.

Others had commented already. Quietly. Carefully.

I think I saw her once too.
She told me I was just difficult.
I never realised it wasn't just me.

And beneath it all, an email address:
truthbeginswithnames@protonmail.com

Something was building. Not a scream — not yet. But a hum. A warning.

Or maybe an uprising.

I sat with the files spread around me like a map of my own silence.

And I finally, fully understood:
This wasn't just about Lily.
Or Marianne.

This was about what happens when someone rewrites the narrative — and no one stops them.

And what happens when, one by one, the ghosts begin to speak.

The Anatomy of Harm

The Email That Opened the Door

The message came at 3:12 a.m.

I was awake. Not from nightmares, but from that particular brand of restlessness that comes when your past has been reanimated and walks the corridors of your home like it never left.

The sender:
truthbeginswithnames@protonmail.com

The subject line:
"I know who she really is."

I clicked it before I could hesitate.

There was no greeting. No sign-off.

Just this:

> *She called herself Marianne Vale when I knew her.*
> *But her name wasn't always that.*
> *I found something you'll want to see.*
> *Do you remember a girl called Naomi Elkins?*
>
> *I think she was the first.*

There was a link beneath the message.
A password-protected folder.

Password: **herliewaslove**

My hands hesitated above the keyboard. Not because I feared what was inside, but because part of me already knew.

There had always been something about Marianne that felt... curated. Like the version of herself she presented to the world had been rehearsed, recited, perfected. Her empathy wasn't fake, exactly — it was *too precise*. Too elegant to be fully real.

Even back then, we whispered about it.

"Is she married?"
"No one's ever met him."
"Where did she train?"
"She says Switzerland."
"What name did she publish under before?"
"Apparently she changed it. Something about privacy."

But the truth is: we didn't ask.

Because no one questions a woman who saves broken people — not until the cracks show.

And by then, it's already too late.

The folder opened to a single file: a scan of a public record.

A name change deed.
Naomi Elkins → Marianne Vale
Dated eleven years ago.

Beneath that, a second file — a clipping from a northern newspaper. Faded, but legible.

"Teen Girl's Death Raises Questions at Residential Programme"
It described a young woman who had died by suicide in a "therapeutic living environment" designed to help troubled girls reintegrate into society. No staff were charged. No one named.

But in the final paragraph, a brief note:

> "One of the senior care staff, a Naomi Elkins (25), has since left the programme and could not be reached for comment."

My stomach turned.

It wasn't just that she had a different name.

It was that she'd *already done this once.*

Another girl.

Another death.

Another institution dissolved under a cloud of ambiguity.

And then: reinvention.

New name. New city. New victims.

I sat back in the chair, blood draining from my face.

Georgia had been right — this wasn't about Marianne *changing*. It was about Marianne *perfecting* the mask.

Refining her tactics. Learning the language of recovery better than anyone else, until she could hide her harm in plain sight.

I forwarded the email to Georgia.

Then I printed the files. Held them in my hands like evidence, like grief.

And I realised something cold and vital:

This wasn't a case of a therapist who got too close.
Or a woman who crossed ethical lines.

This was a pattern.
A method.
A sequence of damage, veiled in therapeutic language and gentle touch.

She hadn't just hurt Lily.

She had *chosen* her.

And now, someone had finally followed the breadcrumb trail all the way back to the start.

A Body Count Without Graves

It's strange, the things you remember once the denial slips.
Not the big moments — not the suicide, or the scandal, or the resignation letters tucked into manila envelopes.
No. What you remember are the *tiny* details.
The things that never quite made sense — but didn't seem worth mentioning at the time.

Like the way Marianne used to hum before sessions.
Always the same melody.
Always just under her breath.
Not loud enough to recognise — but persistent, like a lullaby only she could hear.

Or how she never displayed certificates in her office.
She said it was because she didn't want to "intimidate" the clients.
I'd believed her.

After the email, I stayed awake until dawn. Reading. Re-reading. Cross-referencing timelines.

It lined up.

Naomi Elkins had vanished from public records the year before Marianne appeared at the clinic. Her name had no trace in psychology journals, no published research, no credentials from any UK institution that I could verify.

What she had... was presence.

That unnerving calm. That way of seeing through people like she was reading a case file hidden behind their pupils.

She didn't *need* qualifications.

She had charisma.

And it had worked.

Again, and again, and again.

I compiled a list.

Five names.
Five girls.

1. **Lily Carrick** – age 19. Found dead in her flat, March 2016.

2. **Amara Benton** – age 21. OD'd after leaving a clinic Marianne once guest-lectured at.

3. **Chloe Idris** – age 18. Went missing from a trauma programme. Presumed suicide, body never found.

4. **Romy Sinclair** – age 20. Jumped from a car park rooftop after two months of therapy with "a female trauma expert". No official name given.

5. **Naomi Elkins** – age 15. The girl in the original article. The first.

Five girls.

Five endings.

And no inquests that led anywhere real.

Just careful phrases.
"Vulnerable."
"Unstable."
"Complicated histories."

Georgia replied to my email at 6:01 a.m.

> *Holy shit. I think this is it.*
> *This is what they missed. Or buried. Or let*
> *her walk away from.*
> *I'm going to call someone. Someone who*
> *might actually listen this time.*

Then, another message.

> *Can I come back today?*

I said yes.

But my stomach twisted.

Because the more we uncovered, the more I feared what we still didn't know.

By the time Georgia arrived, I had made copies of everything. Printed, backed up, labelled.

I'd switched on the recorder on my phone — not to trap her, but to *preserve* her. I was becoming paranoid. Paranoia, when it roots deep enough, feels like safety.

She brought more with her — not papers this time, but a photograph. It was folded, soft with age, smudged at the corners.

It showed two girls sitting on a wall in school uniforms. One was Lily. The other — slightly taller, smiling wide — was a girl I didn't recognise.

"This was taken six months before she died," Georgia said. "I think the other girl's name was Imogen. She used to come to the clinic too. I looked her up."

I braced.

"She died last year. In Scotland. Another suicide. Guess who her therapist was?"

I didn't speak.

I couldn't.

Because now we weren't talking about coincidence.

We were talking about a body count.

Unmarked. Unprosecuted. Dismissed as misfortune.

But real.

And if no one stopped her, there would be more.

She Always Left Before the Fire Started

In every place Marianne worked, she left just before things went bad.

A sudden resignation. A "change in focus."

Sometimes the building changed hands. Sometimes it was quietly dissolved.

But the pattern was there, hidden in the paper trail if you knew how to read between lines that were deliberately left faint.

She never left when things *collapsed*.
She left the moment *they might*.

It was her gift — timing.
Disappearing just as the smoke began to curl, so no one noticed she'd been holding the match.

Georgia and I pinned the timeline to the wall.

String, pins, overlapping papers.

It looked like a conspiracy board. Like something you'd mock on a crime drama. But when you stood back and took it all in, it was horrifyingly neat.

There were too many names for a woman with no formal caseload. Too many connections. Too many girls who vanished after "treatment."

"This isn't just negligence," Georgia said, voice tight. "It's predatory."

I nodded.

"She didn't treat trauma. She *sourced* it."

And what's worse — she told us.

Over and over again.

She told us, in lectures and supervision notes, that *some people stay broken because they choose to be*. That it was our job not to coddle them, but to *redirect their story*.

We clapped when she said that.

Because we didn't know it meant *overwrite*.

We thought it meant *empower*.

I remembered a session from years ago. Not with a client. With Marianne.

A supervision, late evening, wine on her desk — not enough to report, just enough to feel intimate.

We were discussing Lily.

"She's forming unhealthy attachments," I'd said. "She keeps asking to see my notes. She thinks I know something about her life that she doesn't."

And Marianne had smiled, slow and deliberate.

"She's not asking you for notes, Eve. She's asking for confirmation. That her story matters. That it happened the way she remembers."

She sipped her wine.

"If you really want to help her… make her forget."

At the time, I'd thought it was a metaphor. A comment about therapeutic detachment.

Now I wasn't so sure.

Georgia tapped a file. "We need someone else. Someone outside of us. Police, press, anyone."

"No police will listen without a formal complaint," I said. "And most journalists won't print it unless there's a name."

"I'll use mine."

I looked at her.

She was young. Not naive, but still burningly righteous. The kind of righteousness I'd once had, before I learned how tightly systems closed around themselves.

"She'll come for you," I said.

"I hope she does," Georgia replied. "At least then someone might believe me."

Later that night, after Georgia left, I walked out to the cliff's edge behind the house.

I used to come here to breathe.

Now it just felt like a ledge between two truths — the one I'd lived with, and the one I was finally naming.

The wind whipped my coat around me like a warning.

And in that moment, I understood what made Marianne so terrifying.

It wasn't that she lied.

It was that she made you believe *you were the one misremembering*.

The next morning, I received an envelope.

Handwritten. No stamp.

Inside: a photograph of my old office, burnt out, windows smashed.

And on the back, a sentence scrawled in red pen:

"You always knew how to start a fire, Eve."

The Manipulator's Mirror

I stared at the photo for nearly an hour.

Not because it shocked me — not exactly. But because it proved something I'd never wanted to admit:
Someone was watching. Not from afar. Not digitally. *Physically*.

They had been here.

Near the house.
Near me.

The photograph wasn't just a threat.

It was an echo.

The image showed the charred remains of the clinic office I'd once worked in. It had been derelict for years, shut down after Lily's death and a slow internal unravelling of staff.

But the photograph wasn't old.

The soot was fresh. The window edges jagged. The fire recent.

I checked the local news. Nothing.

Of course not.

Small fires in abandoned buildings don't make headlines.

Unless you know what they used to hold.

Unless you're the one who lit it.

I turned the photo over again.
You always knew how to start a fire, Eve.

A sentence that worked like glass — every word sharp.

Was it literal? Metaphorical? Was I being accused?

Or worse — was it a reminder?

Because that phrase wasn't new.

Marianne had said it once, in supervision, years ago, smiling like it was a compliment:

> "You know how to start a fire, Eve. You just don't always stay to watch it burn."

It had made me laugh then.

Now it made my blood run cold.

I walked back through every file we'd compiled. Every article, every note, every overlapping trauma.
Trying to understand what she wanted.

Control? Revenge?
To silence us?

No — it was more surgical than that.

Marianne never punished.
She *recalibrated*.

When something threatened her structure, she didn't dismantle it — she rewrote the story around it until it couldn't speak anymore.

I knew the playbook. She'd taught it to me.

Reframing. Deflection. Gaslighting by language.
We were trained to call it *narrative therapy*.
She used it to erase people.

That night, I sat on the floor with the photo, the files, and my old dictaphone — the one I hadn't used since I left the profession.

There were only a few old recordings left. Most were clinical. Benign. Forgettable.

But one…
One was marked with a date that stopped me.

March 16th, 2016.

The day before Lily died.

My hand hovered over the play button.

Pressed.

[Soft static. Shuffling.]

Marianne's voice, sharp, composed:
"You mustn't tell Eve. She doesn't understand where this leads."

Lily's voice, soft, muffled:
"She thinks you care about me."

Marianne again:
"I *do* care about you, Lily. I care enough to push you out of the story you've trapped yourself in."

[Pause]

Lily:
"What if the story *is* true?"

Marianne:
"Then we change the ending."

Click.

I dropped the recorder.

Because I'd heard enough.

Because that was the moment it became undeniable:
Marianne *had* manipulated Lily.
Not just as a therapist, but as an architect of her reality.
She'd offered help and handed her a noose disguised as narrative closure.

I emailed the file to Georgia.

Subject: **You need to hear this.**

Then, another message:

> *We can't do this quietly anymore.*
> *She doesn't deserve that courtesy.*

My phone buzzed again — a new message.
From an unknown number.

This time, just one line.

> *You still don't understand what she's capable*
> *of, do you?*

What She Left Out of the Records

In therapy, they tell you the most dangerous patients are the ones who know how to tell their story well.
The ones who know how to cry in the right places.
Pause in the right silences.
Use just enough vulnerability to make you feel needed.

But they never warn you about the therapists who do it too.

I stayed awake again. Not from fear. From preparation.

There's a kind of energy that takes over once you accept war is coming — not the kind with blood and noise, but with emails, character assassinations, and thinly veiled legal threats.

Marianne wouldn't come for me with fists.

She'd come with *doubt*.

And it had already begun.

At 3:27 a.m., Georgia forwarded a message from her personal inbox.

It was from an anonymous account, but the language was unmistakable.

>*Dear Georgia,

>Be careful who you trust.
>Eve Whitaker has a long history of crossing

professional boundaries.
She was involved in a disciplinary case long before Lily Carrick.
Perhaps you should ask her about the Hastings Centre incident.

You're being used.

Some women are broken for a reason.

—A Concerned Colleague*

There it was.

The twist of the knife.

Because the Hastings Centre incident was real.

And I'd never told Georgia. Or anyone.

It happened two years before I met Marianne.

During my first post-graduate placement. Fresh, eager, idealistic.

There was a patient — Rachel. Twenty-four. Childhood trauma. Dissociative episodes. No diagnosis had ever stuck.

We bonded too quickly.

She began writing me letters between sessions. Told me I was the first person who'd ever seen her. I was flattered

— inexperienced enough to believe that was a sign I was doing well.

Then one day, she showed up outside the clinic.

Waited for me to finish.
Held a letter in her hand.
Said it was her final goodbye.

I stopped her. Called the crisis team. Stayed with her until help arrived.

And in the days that followed, I was quietly removed from her case.

Not because I'd done anything *wrong*, but because the bond had blurred. Because the institution feared liability more than it feared losing her trust.

I wasn't formally disciplined.

But the message was clear: *you were too close.*

I told myself, after that, I'd never make the same mistake.

And then came Marianne.

Who praised closeness. Who encouraged fusion. Who rewarded emotional proximity with power.

I didn't realise until too late that she'd found me at my most vulnerable.
Not because I was unqualified — but because I was

already bleeding.
And she made it feel like therapy.

The email Georgia received was more than a warning.

It was a scalpel.

Because it wasn't meant to expose me — it was meant to *destabilise* her.

Make her question the person she'd trusted. Make her hesitate.

But Georgia…
Georgia didn't flinch.

She forwarded me the message with a single note:

> *Is this true? Doesn't change a thing. But I'd rather hear it from you.*

And so I told her.

All of it.

Not to defend myself — but to *remove the weapon* from Marianne's hands.

That morning, Georgia made the first public post.

A tweet.

Plain. Unflinching.

My sister Lily died during "trauma therapy"
with a woman named Marianne Vale.
We've found other victims.
If you knew her — as a therapist, a mentor, or
anything else — please come forward.

You're not alone.

#TheLieShePromised

By noon, it had over 3,000 shares.

By evening, messages began flooding in.

Some angry. Some terrified.
But many… relieved.

> *"I thought it was just me."*
> *"She ruined me."*
> *"I still hear her voice when I try to sleep."*

And then, finally, one voice I hadn't expected.

An email.

From a former colleague. From inside the clinic.

Subject: **I saw what she did. I can help you prove it.**

The Testimony They Never Took

The One Who Stayed Silent Then

Her name was Dr Harriet Bowen.

I hadn't thought about her in years.

She'd worked beside Marianne in the final six months of the clinic's operation — brought in, I suspect now, to give the place a sense of structure. She'd always seemed too careful, too measured for the chaos around her. The kind of professional who lived inside ethical frameworks, who never spoke a word out of place.

Which is probably why she lasted.

And why she said nothing — until now.

Her email arrived at 6:42 a.m.

> *Eve,
>
> I saw your name on the Twitter thread. I've kept quiet for years, partly out of fear, partly because I convinced myself I hadn't seen enough.
> But I did.
>
> I saw how she worked with Lily. I knew it wasn't right.

I tried to raise concerns once. I was shut down.
They told me she was "managing complex transferences" — and that I didn't understand the dynamic.

I did.
That was the problem.*

*She was orchestrating dependency.

I have notes.
Contemporaneous. Kept privately.

I will give them to you. But I can't be seen.
Not yet.*

H.

I reread it three times before forwarding it to Georgia.

Then I sat back in my chair and let the guilt rise like steam.

Because I remembered the staff meeting Harriet referenced.

I'd been there.
I'd heard her try.
I'd watched Marianne discredit her with one softly spoken line:

"Harriet's always been cautious — it's part of her charm."

And we laughed.

We laughed because we wanted to believe Marianne was in control.
Because to challenge her was to dismantle the entire illusion.

And because we didn't want to see what Harriet saw.

Harriet agreed to meet me, anonymously.

Not in a café. Not even in public.

She suggested a church hall — disused on weekdays, rented by a community counselling service where she still volunteered once a week.

Neutral ground.

The kind of place where confession lives without judgment.

When I arrived, she was already there.

Still composed. Still restrained. But thinner. Tired in a way that went beyond sleep.

She didn't greet me with small talk.

Just a plain brown envelope and a single line:

"You were the one she trained to replace her, you know."

I flinched. "What?"

Harriet nodded slowly. "She was grooming you. Not sexually. Not even emotionally — not directly. But professionally. She saw something in you. Obedience. Loyalty. The capacity to do what she did. Better, even. And when Lily died, you cracked."

"That's not—"

She held up a hand. "It's not an accusation. It's a mercy. You cracked. You left. That's what saved you."

I looked down at the envelope. "And these?"

"Session logs. Observations. Things I was never asked to submit because I was removed from Lily's care. But I kept them. For this."

I opened the envelope right there.

Inside, a dozen pages. Scanned, annotated, dated.

One in particular made me stop breathing.

It was a typed transcript — a conversation Harriet had observed between Lily and Marianne from the other side of the mirror.

Lily: "You don't believe me."

Marianne: "I believe you're hurting."

Lily: "But not what caused it."

Marianne: "Does it matter? Pain is pain. We can rewrite the origin if it's not useful anymore."

Lily: "But it happened."

Marianne: "Then let's pretend it didn't. Just for today. See how that feels."

I handed the page back.

Harriet didn't take it.

"Keep it," she said. "Use it. Or don't. But don't pretend anymore that she didn't train you in her image."

Later, as I left, Harriet touched my arm — the only physical contact of the entire meeting.

"Eve," she said, "you were her favourite because you knew how to stay quiet. You'll be dangerous now because you've stopped."

And then she walked away.

Not a goodbye. Just gone.

I returned home with shaking hands, the envelope pressed against my chest like a heartbeat.

Inside were the words Lily never got to use as evidence.

The words no one wanted to hear when she was alive.

The words that might finally make someone listen.

The Building of a Case No One Asked For

The envelope sat on the kitchen table like an open wound.

Pages half-spilled, annotations underlined in blue, each line bleeding with what no one had wanted to say out loud.

Marianne hadn't broken the law.

That was the problem.

She'd broken people.

And there's no section in the criminal code for psychological erasure performed behind a therapist's smile.

Georgia arrived just after noon, face flushed, eyes alive with the kind of fury I recognised in myself now. She'd printed the tweet thread. Highlighted names. Created a spreadsheet.

"They're coming forward," she said. "It's happening."

She dropped her bag and began pacing.

"Fourteen messages since last night. All women. All with the same story — they trusted her, and she turned them against themselves."

I handed her Harriet's envelope.

She stopped pacing.

"Are you serious?"

I nodded. "Contemporaneous notes. Detailed. Observed from inside the room."

Georgia sat, almost reverently, and began to read.

Half an hour passed without either of us speaking.

Finally, she said, "This is enough, isn't it? Enough to get someone to act?"

I wanted to believe that.

But I'd seen the way institutions closed ranks.
How the language of liability rewrote trauma into inconvenience.
How girls like Lily became footnotes before the ink on their intake forms had dried.

"It's enough for *us*," I said. "Maybe not yet for the system. But enough to start."

Georgia looked up. "Then let's start."

We called in favours.

Georgia knew someone at a mid-tier paper — a journalist who'd covered institutional abuse before. Her name was **Freya Morton**. Tenacious. Former social worker. Known for printing stories no one else would touch.

We met her at a pub on the edge of London, all dark wood and stained-glass windows. The kind of place where you could whisper without being overheard.

Freya ordered coffee. No alcohol. "Clarity over comfort," she said.

We gave her the files. The recordings. The printouts. The timeline.

And then we told her everything.

She didn't interrupt once.

When we were done, she leaned back, her jaw tight.

"Do you have victims willing to be named?"

"Some," Georgia said. "Not all. Yet."

"Does Marianne Vale know you're doing this?"

I nodded.

Freya paused. "Then I need to ask the ugly question. What are you prepared to risk?"

Georgia didn't blink. "Everything."

I said nothing. Because the answer was the same — but heavier in me.

Freya stood. "I'll do it. But I'll need three days. To verify, to source, to get legal clearance. And I can't promise it'll stay quiet once I start calling people."

She looked at me directly.

"She'll come for you first. You know that, don't you?"

"I'm counting on it," I said.

Back at the house, Georgia fell asleep on the sofa, her arms curled around a cushion, phone in hand. I covered her with a blanket and watched her breathe.

She reminded me of Lily — not in looks, but in spirit.
The same wild hope. The same fury disguised as softness.

And maybe that's why Marianne had chosen Lily.

Because girls like her don't just *feel* pain — they *absorb* it.

Until it becomes too much.

My phone buzzed.

An email.

From: Marianne Vale
Subject: This won't end the way you think.

No body text. No attachment.

Just that line.

I deleted it.

Then opened the recorder app on my phone and hit record.

"My name is Dr Eve Whitaker.

And this is everything I never said —
about Marianne Vale,
about Lily Carrick,
and about the lie we were all told to believe."

The Woman Behind the Curtain

The next morning, the internet changed.

Not all of it — just the corners that mattered. The ones where whispered names catch fire. Survivor forums. Niche Twitter threads. Private Facebook groups where former patients pass around warnings like talismans.

Freya's article had gone live.

"The Therapist Who Rewrote Her Clients: Allegations of Manipulation and Harm Behind the Mask of Healing"

It wasn't sensationalised. It didn't need to be. It simply laid out the facts:

- A series of unexplained deaths.

- A woman who changed her name before launching a new career.

- A pattern of therapy sessions that blurred the line between treatment and control.

- And testimonies — real, raw, recorded.

Mine. Georgia's. Harriet's.

And one anonymous source, who had written:

> *"She told me I was the problem. That I was addicted to my trauma.*

So I spent three years trying to amputate parts of myself to be someone she would approve of.
When I left, I didn't even know who I was anymore."

It spread slowly at first — not viral, not explosive — but with the eerie quiet of something true. Something buried for too long.

And then the responses came.

First: disbelief.
Then: rage.
Then — worse than either — recognition.

> *"This woman was my therapist."*
> *"She destroyed my sister."*
> *"I've been waiting years for someone to say her name."*

And finally:

> *"She's still practicing. Under a new name."*

I froze.

Georgia called me three times before I picked up.

"She's in Bristol," she said. "She's moved again. She's using the name Dr Marie North. Freelance trauma specialist. She runs private retreats for women 'seeking emotional reclamation.'"

She sent the link.

It was all there — a polished website, testimonials (eerily familiar in tone), and a smiling headshot with softer hair and a new surname.

But the eyes were the same.

Still calculating.

Still unblinking.

I stared at the screen and thought of Lily.

How she'd tried so hard to be good.
How she'd moulded herself into Marianne's theories.
How she died not because she was weak — but because she'd *trusted*.

And I thought of all the others who had trusted since.

"We have to stop her," I said.

Georgia nodded through the phone. "We will."

But even as she said it, I felt it.

The shift.

This wasn't a story anymore. It was a *hunt*.

And somewhere, behind another name, another pair of false credentials, Marianne was already rewriting her ending.

That night, I received a voicemail.

Blocked number. No transcription.

Just a recording. One minute and thirteen seconds long.

Marianne's voice. Soft. Affectionate.

> "I see you're still trying to be the hero.
> Still misremembering the details.
>
> You were never innocent, Eve.
> You just hid it better."
>
> [Pause]
>
> "You think you've exposed me. But all you've
> done is confirm your own guilt.
>
> Don't forget —
>
> I taught you everything you know."

I sat on the floor and let the silence return.

But this time, I didn't crumble.

Because this time, the silence wasn't mine.

It was hers.

Breaking.

The Girl in the Mirror

There's a moment when a lie breaks — not cleanly, but like a slow splinter through glass.
Not one sharp noise. Just the sound of everything shifting.

That's what it felt like in the days after the article.

Not justice. Not peace.

Just the gentle, devastating undoing of the silence she'd orchestrated so perfectly.

Three more women came forward publicly.
One from her early days in Manchester.
One from a wellness centre in Edinburgh.
One who had been a teenager when she first met Marianne under the guise of 'mentorship.'

Each story different in shape — but cut from the same bone.

> She isolated me from my friends.
> She told me my mother was the real abuser.
> She called me brave, then punished me for crying.
> She said if I told anyone, no one would believe me.
> She said I needed to hurt in order to heal.

Words like a template. A ritual.

A pattern she'd perfected.

Georgia built a dossier.

Not just of survivors, but of *evidence*.
She'd always had the mind of a lawyer, even if she hadn't followed that path.
Emails. Timelines. Mismatched qualifications. Voicemails. Sessions recorded without consent, but protected by whistleblower laws.

We met with Freya again.

She introduced us to someone she trusted — a legal contact who specialised in psychological malpractice.

The process had begun.

An inquiry. A submission. A case file that now had teeth.

But the hardest part came quietly.

In the form of an envelope.

Sent from a return address in Devon.
Typed. Neat.
Inside: a single photograph.

A girl — around fourteen — in a white jumper, staring into a mirror.

At first, I didn't understand.

Then I looked closer.

The girl wasn't the focus. The mirror was.

Because in the reflection, just behind her —
Was Marianne.

Smiling.

Watching.

Georgia looked at the photo for a long time.

Then said, "How many, Eve?"

"I don't know."

She swallowed hard. "Do you think she started with Lily?"

"No," I said. "I think Lily was the first one who ever resisted."

I began drafting a statement.

For the inquiry. For the survivors. For the woman I had once been — the one who had sat beside Marianne and called it learning.

> *"I believed her because she knew how to sound like truth.
>
> I watched her wound girls and call it treatment.
>
> I listened to her dismiss pain as performance.

I helped build the lie — even when it didn't feel right — because I thought it was the only way to belong.

And I stayed silent because she told me the silence was kindness."*

That night, Georgia cried.

Not loudly. Not performatively.

Just quietly, on the edge of the sofa, like someone trying to grieve something they never got to hold.

"I feel like she killed her all over again," she said.

And I knew who she meant.

Not just Lily. But every girl who walked into a room wanting help and left with their voice hollowed out.

I sat beside her and whispered what I should have said years ago:

"She didn't deserve that ending."

"No," Georgia said. "But maybe… we can still change the story."

And somewhere, deep inside me, a question stirred.

One I hadn't let surface since the very beginning.

What if I was the only one who ever got close enough
to stop her —
and I never tried?

The Reckoning Begins Quietly

The official notice came two days later.

A stamped letter from the **Health and Care Professions Council (HCPC)**.

Formal language. Passive voice.

They were opening a preliminary investigation into Dr Marie North — formerly known as Marianne Vale, formerly known as Naomi Elkins.

The letter didn't say much. But it said enough.

It was beginning.

Not just the reckoning.

The *recording* of what had been ignored.

Georgia brought cake.

It was absurd, and perfect.

We didn't eat it. Just let it sit between us on the coffee table like a quiet symbol of survival.

"I thought we'd feel triumphant," she said. "I thought I'd scream or throw my arms up or cry in a film-worthy way."

I smiled. "Me too."

Instead, we sat in silence, shoulders brushing. Not victory, not relief — just something more honest.

Exhaustion.
Tenderness.
And a strange, careful kind of peace.

My inbox was full of names I didn't recognise.

Some were reporters.

Some were survivors.

One was a girl who had never spoken before, who simply wrote:

> *I thought she was my lifeline.
> But she was the one holding the weight that dragged me under.
>
> Thank you for pulling me out.*

I didn't reply right away.
Because there are no words that can fix what was done.
Only words that say: *I believe you. I see you. It wasn't your fault.*

And that's what I sent.

Then came a voicemail from Freya.

"Brace yourself."

I pressed play.

*"We've just confirmed she's fled.
The clinic's been cleared out. The phone disconnected. Website offline.

But there's more."*

A pause.

> *"She's filed a formal complaint against you, Eve. Claims of defamation.*
> *She's saying you were the one with an inappropriate attachment to Lily.*
> *That you manipulated records to frame her."*

I sank into the chair, breath caught mid-chest.

Of course she had.

Because this wasn't just about survival.

It was about *control*.

And Marianne never lost control. She just changed the story.

That night, I printed everything.

Every email. Every photograph. Every file Georgia and I had gathered. I organised it, indexed it, and made three separate copies.

Not because I was afraid she'd win.

But because I knew she wouldn't go down without taking a few truths with her.

When I finally slept, I dreamed of Lily.

She was standing in the corridor of the old clinic, rain trickling down the windows, her hoodie pulled over her head.

I walked toward her.

She turned to face me.

And she said:

"Tell them it mattered."

I woke at 4:17 a.m., tears dry on my cheeks.

I wrote the words on a post-it and stuck it above my desk.

It mattered.

Because it did.

Because it does.

Because she mattered.

The Stories She Stole

The Girls She Made into Fiction

There are different kinds of theft.

The theft of time.
The theft of innocence.
The theft of safety.

But what Marianne did — what Naomi did, what Marie North tried to keep doing — was more precise.

She stole *narrative*.

She took girls who were half-formed in their pain and rewrote them. Turned trauma into theatre. Shaped them into characters in her own therapeutic mythology.

And when they no longer fit the story, she discarded them.

Like plot lines that had lost their use.

In the files Georgia and I had gathered, there was a pattern to her notes — a language she used over and over, no matter the patient.

"Seeks attention."
"Immersed in victim identity."
"Unable to maintain objective memory."
"Responsive to containment."
"Displays learned helplessness."

Cold phrases.

Clinical, detached — and yet they whispered her obsession with power.

Each girl's history flattened into a single shape: malleable. Breakable.

And each time, she was the one holding the scalpel.

I reread Lily's notes again.

Not the ones Marianne wrote. The ones Lily left in her journal, later found among her belongings — now sent to us by Georgia's father, after months of resistance.

One entry was dated a week before her death.

> *I feel like a puppet. Not even a broken one. Just a quiet one.
>
> Every time I try to speak, I hear her voice in my mouth instead.
>
> She says I'm finally making progress. But I think I'm just becoming more like her.*

I traced the words with my fingertip.

And I wondered how many other girls had written something similar — and burned it, or hidden it, or whispered it into pillows before falling asleep in houses where no one ever knew what happened behind the therapy room door.

Georgia started mapping them — the women who came forward after the article, and the ones who had been there from the start. Some were teenagers then, now mothers themselves. Some had attempted to forget. Others hadn't been able to.

But they all described the same thing.

> "She mirrored me until I didn't know who I was."
> "She was the only one I trusted. And then she turned that against me."
> "She gave me permission to blame myself."

We gave them codenames at first. For privacy. For protection.

But then something changed.

One woman — Rachel, 38 — emailed and said,

> "Use my name.
> She made me invisible long enough."

So we stopped hiding them.

Not recklessly. But carefully.
Names shared with consent.
Voices finally claiming authorship of their own story again.

We made a list.
Printed it.
Pinned it to the wall of my kitchen.

By the time we reached twenty-three names, we had to start a second page.

One of the most recent entries came from a woman in Wales.

She'd been a patient at a retreat led by "Dr Marie North" just seven months earlier.

She wrote:

> *"I thought she was saving me.
> But every time I disagreed, she smiled like I was being difficult.
>
> She told me I had a choice: stay in my pain or step into her method.
>
> And when I cried, she said crying was resistance.
> That it meant I wasn't ready to be well."*

That line sat with me.

Crying is resistance.

What an insidious way to frame someone's grief.

Georgia placed a post-it on the map we were building.
It read simply:

"This is not therapy. This is narrative warfare."

And it was.

Because what Marianne had done — what she continued to do, until the last retreat fell apart — was erase the *real story* each girl brought into the room.

She replaced it with one of her own design.

A story where she was the saviour.

And they were too fragile to ever understand the truth.

But they understood now.

And they were done being characters in her book.

They were writing their own.

The Anatomy of Her Method

The inquiry team called it "a troubling trend of unethical practice."

A euphemism, like all things official.
Words polished until they no longer cut.

But Georgia and I had no need for euphemisms.

We had a name for it.

The Method.

It wasn't written down anywhere — Marianne was far too careful for that.
But it revealed itself in the transcripts, in the echoes between survivors' words.

A predictable choreography of control.

It went like this:

Step 1: Isolation
Subtle at first.
"You don't need their validation."
"Your family never understood your pain."
"They're triggering your regressions."

A slow uncoupling from reality — until the only person left with any insight into your trauma was Marianne.

And when you resisted?

She called it *clinging to the past.*

Step 2: Reframing

This was where she truly excelled.

She'd take your worst memory and retell it with just enough empathy to make you trust her.

Then, slowly, she'd reframe it.

> "Perhaps it didn't happen the way you remember."
> "Memory is shaped by emotion, not accuracy."
> "What if your abuser wasn't cruel, just wounded?"

She'd offer relief. Not healing.

Permission to doubt yourself.

And you took it, because what she offered next was even more intoxicating.

Step 3: Reinvention

Once you were untethered, she helped you rebuild.

But only in her image.

Words like "resilience," "emotional elevation," "post-traumatic insight."

You were praised for progress, but punished for pain.

Crying too often was regression.
Anger was resistance.
Asking questions? *A barrier to growth.*

By the end, you were no longer you.

You were a mirror of her — calm, articulate, unshaken.

Until you weren't.

Until something cracked.

Until the grief slipped through anyway.

And then came the final step.

Step 4: Erasure

Some were ghosted.

Others were gently removed.

A few — like Lily — were marked as "non-compliant" and referred elsewhere.

But the end was always the same.

Once your pain no longer served her narrative, you were discarded.

And if you broke?

It was proof the work hadn't been finished.

Not her failure — yours.

Georgia pinned the four steps above the map.

Isolation. Reframing. Reinvention. Erasure.

We stared at them for a long time.

Then she said, "It's like cult methodology, hidden in counselling language."

And it was.

Because Marianne didn't just steal stories.

She *reconstructed* them.

So cleanly, so convincingly, that even the survivors struggled to recognise what had been taken.

I found an old notebook from my final year of training.

Inside, a quote I'd copied from one of Marianne's lectures:

> *"The wounded become narrators. The healed become editors."*

At the time, I'd underlined it.
I thought it was profound.

Now it made me nauseous.

We decided to send everything — the map, the method, the testimonies — to the inquiry team.

No redactions. No apologies.

Freya warned us:
"It might not be admissible in a courtroom. But it'll be impossible to ignore."

That was enough.

Because we didn't want revenge.

We wanted *record*.

We wanted *witness*.

And slowly, the tide began to turn.

Therapists began commenting under the article.
Ethics boards quietly opened side discussions.
A podcast invited Georgia to speak.

A national helpline reported an uptick in calls referencing "unorthodox therapy methods."

They didn't say her name.

But we knew.

She was losing control of the narrative.

And for the first time in over a decade…

She wasn't the one writing it.

The Woman Without a Past

She vanished the day before the first official hearing.

Not in a dramatic way.

There was no headline. No chase. No press conference.

Just a quiet withdrawal.

Her website disappeared.
The social media accounts went dark.
Emails bounced. Phone numbers disconnected.

A few clients reported last-minute cancellations. One said she left a voicemail apologising for "a family emergency abroad."

But we knew better.

Marianne hadn't fled because she was scared of punishment.

She'd fled because she could no longer control the story.

And that, for someone like her, is the real death sentence.

Georgia cried.

Not because we'd lost.

But because it felt unfinished.

Like watching a house burn down and never seeing the body inside.

"We were supposed to stop her," she said. "Not just expose her. *Stop her.*"

"We did," I said. "We stopped the version of her that lived in the light. What comes next… won't be as easy for her to build."

But I wasn't as sure as I sounded.

Because women like Marianne don't disappear.

They *recur.*

That evening, I received a parcel.

No return address.

Inside, a single book.

Marianne's unpublished manuscript:
"The Reclaimed Self: A Journey Beyond Trauma"

A note tucked inside read:

> *You wanted my truth.
> So here it is.
>
> — M.*

I held it for hours before I opened it.

Every page was poison dressed in poetry.

Self-help reframed as scripture. Therapy language weaponised until you could no longer tell where guidance ended and coercion began.

And threaded throughout, references to an unnamed former colleague.

> "She misunderstood the work.
> She became attached to her own saviour complex.
> She betrayed not just me, but the patients we were saving together."

She was rewriting me now.

I didn't burn the book.

I logged it.

Scanned it.

Archived it.

Because even monsters deserve footnotes.

And because I knew the final story would be ours to write — not hers.

Georgia and I met with Freya one last time.

We handed over everything.

Not because we wanted another article, but because we wanted *record*.

A public archive. A place survivors could point to and say: "There. That's what happened."

We left the last folder open on the table.

Inside, Lily's photo.

The real one.

The one where she's smiling, unscripted. Wind in her hair. No therapy room in sight.

We didn't say goodbye.

We just walked away.

What They Remember of Her Now

Marianne Vale no longer exists.
Not officially.
Not online.
Not in the registries she once so carefully manipulated.

But her shadow lingers — not in headlines, but in the minds of those she left behind.

You can still hear her name in the hesitant voices of support groups.
You can still trace her method in the anxious retellings of therapy gone wrong.
You can still feel her presence in the language survivors use:

> *I thought it was my fault.*
> *She made me believe I was lying.*
> *It took years to unlearn her voice.*

She's no longer working, but her legacy haunts the places she touched.

Because the wounds she created weren't visible.

They were *narrative wounds* — the kind that rot beneath the surface.

Georgia kept going.

After the hearings. After the inquiry closed its first chapter.
She built a platform. Quietly. Carefully.
A survivor-led network for those manipulated by

professionals who blurred lines, stole autonomy, rewrote history.

She called it *The Story You Were Told*.

It wasn't a charity. Not yet.
But it was something.

A place where the erased could speak.
Where girls like Lily had their names returned.

I remained quieter.

I wasn't a campaigner.

I was a witness.
And maybe that was enough.

I went back to writing — not reports, not case notes.

Just truth.

Fiction, sometimes, but laced with real grief.
The kind that gives itself away in dialogue.
The kind that bleeds into character like memory.

One story — a short piece about a girl who was never believed — was picked up by a small press.

They asked if it was based on anyone real.

I said no.

But I thought of Lily.

And how much she'd hated mirrors.

The final thing that came — months later — was a letter.

Handwritten. No signature.

The handwriting was eerily neat. Familiar.

Inside:

> *You win.*
>
> *But you always needed to.*
>
> *That's what made you easy to mould.*
>
> *— M*

Georgia wanted to hand it to the police.
I said no.

Because it wasn't a threat.

It was a *relapse*.

The voice of a woman who no longer had a captive audience.

Just echoes.

And ghosts.

I pinned it to the wall behind my desk. Not as a trophy. As a reminder.

That the most dangerous people aren't the loud ones.

They're the ones who whisper so well, you forget your own voice.

The Lie She Promised

There was never just one lie.

Not really.

Marianne didn't offer deception in a single sentence or a single act.

She offered it like comfort.
Layered. Warm. Intimate.

> *You're special.*
> *They won't understand you like I do.*
> *You're healing faster than you realise.*
> *Let me help you forget.*

But beneath all of it, the deepest lie she promised — the one that unravelled the most — was this:

That pain makes you pliable.

And for a time, she was right.

Because pain does make you soft.
It opens you.
It leaves you looking for shape, for narrative, for rescue.

She stepped into that space like she'd been rehearsing her whole life.

But pain is not permission.
And survival is not silence.

And girls like Lily — and Georgia — and even me —

We don't stay pliable.

We remember.

And we speak.

And we *write*.

In the end, the lie she promised was the same lie all manipulators whisper:

> *This story only belongs to me.*

But she was wrong.

It belongs to every woman she tried to overwrite.

Every girl she called dramatic.

Every survivor who thought they were broken beyond repair.

Every soul she dismissed with a clinical smile and an empty metaphor.

And if there is justice — if not in courtrooms, then in quiet homes and bookmarked pages and whispered names reclaimed —
it is this:

> That she didn't get the final chapter.
> We did.

The Memory That
Fought to Survive

The House That Held Too Many Secrets

It began with a smell.

The house where it had all started — the original clinic — was due for demolition.
A local housing development had bought the land.
They were tearing it down to build flats.
Affordable, ironically.

But a structural engineer had gone in one final time, and noticed something.
A lingering scent of burning.

They thought it was from the fire earlier that year — the one we never quite confirmed, the one we suspected was staged.
But this was different.

It led them to a room that hadn't been listed on any original plans.

A small, sealed office in the basement.

Inside:

- A filing cabinet with scorched edges

- A broken recorder

- A single chair

- And one photograph
  Pinned to the wall.

The photo was of me.

Taken from behind, blurred, low light — likely through a pane of glass.

I was seated. Pen in hand. Mid-session.

I stared at it for a long time when they emailed it to me.

The timestamp matched a week before Lily's death.

I don't remember that photo being taken.
I don't remember the angle.
But I remember the feeling:
Being watched even when I thought I was alone.

Georgia stood behind me, reading the email over my shoulder.

"That's not just surveillance," she said. "That's obsession."

We requested access to the rest of the recovered contents.

Much had been destroyed by smoke and damp.

But the recorder still held a fragment — one surviving audio file.

I played it.

> [Static. Then voices.]

Marianne:

> *"Sometimes the best way to remember is to agree to forget. Do you understand?"*

A pause.

Lily:

> *"I don't want to forget."*

Marianne:

> *"But forgetting is healing."*

Lily:

> *"No. It's silence."*

Then nothing.

Just silence.

I took the audio to the inquiry team.

They filed it.

Marked it.

But still, they said:

"It may not be admissible."

Because that's what institutions do.
They catalogue pain, but rarely act on it.

Georgia said we needed something louder.

So we made it public.

Not the whole audio. Just the quote.

Lily's voice.

Clear. Defiant.

No. It's silence.

We printed it on posters.
Shared it on forums.
Published it in the epilogue of Freya's second piece.

And survivors everywhere understood what it meant.

Lily had never forgotten.
Even when they told her to.
Even when I did.

Her memory had fought to survive.

Not in court.

Not in files.

But in *us*.

In Georgia.
In every girl who finally said, *that happened to me too.*

There's power in being remembered.
Even when you're gone.

Especially when you're gone.

Because to be remembered *honestly* —
not as a symbol, not as a headline,
but as a full human being —
is the one thing they can never take from you.

Not even Marianne.

The Legacy They Tried to Control

Some names vanish.

Not because they're forgotten — but because they've been *scrubbed*.

That's what happened to "Dr Marie North."

Once the inquiry gained traction, her listings were delisted.
Her profiles purged.
Her content flagged and quietly removed under "professional misrepresentation."

No formal charges were brought.
But the system began to close its doors.

A late apology from a private regulation body came months after the fact.

> *"We regret that our oversight may have contributed to avoidable distress."*

Avoidable distress.

Two words that felt like an obituary in disguise.

Georgia and I didn't hold a celebration.
We didn't need to.

The real vindication came in the emails.
In the quiet messages from women who no longer whispered.

"I've started therapy again. With someone safe this time."
"I told my sister what really happened. She believed me."
"I wrote a piece for my local paper. I signed my name."

Every one of them was a quiet undoing.
Of what Marianne had silenced.
Of what I had, at one time, enabled through fear.

I found myself going back to the house — the clinic — one final time before the demolition.

There was no sign of her left.
No smell. No echo.
Just the shape of something that used to take and take and take.

I walked the halls alone.
No Georgia. No voice recorder.
Just me.

And I stood in the room where I used to sit with Lily, beneath that mirror we never dared to look directly into. The one-way glass.

It was smashed now.

But the frame still hung — empty, but intact.

And I realised:

This is what she feared most.

Not exposure.
Not even justice.

But *reflection*.

The kind that doesn't distort.
The kind that shows you exactly what you did.

I took a shard of the mirror with me.
Wrapped it in tissue.
Put it in a drawer.

Not as a keepsake.

As a reminder.

That even the sharpest stories can crack.

That night, Georgia and I drank cheap wine from mugs.

We laughed.
Real, exhausted laughter.
The kind that only comes once the storm has passed and the roof still holds.

"Do you think she's still out there?" she asked.

I didn't answer for a long time.

Then said:

"Maybe. But if she is — she's finally looking over her shoulder."

Georgia smiled.
Raised her mug.

"To the girls who didn't stay quiet."

"To the story that outlived her," I replied.

And we drank.

Rewriting the Ending

For months, I avoided writing the book.

Not the one you're reading now — the real one. The one they asked me to write after the case closed.
A publisher reached out. Offered an advance. Called it *"a rare opportunity to educate and empower."*

It made me feel sick.

Because I didn't want to capitalise on pain.
Especially not pain I'd once helped mute.

But Georgia said something that changed my mind.

> "If *she* gets to publish her version, you damn well better publish yours."

And so, I did.

It wasn't easy.

I started with facts, but it felt cold.
I tried memoir, but it felt self-indulgent.
I wrote Lily's name fifty times before I let myself include it in the first sentence.

In the end, it wasn't about Marianne.

Not really.

It was about silence.
And what happens when it's broken.

It was about narrative — how easily it can be weaponised.
And how fiercely it must be reclaimed.

The book was small.
Not a bestseller.
But it found its way.

Therapists emailed me.
Not to condemn, but to thank me.

> "You reminded me to check my power."
> "I've restructured how I approach trauma clients."
> "I've started asking if they feel heard — really heard."

Survivors wrote too.

Some angry.
Some grateful.
Some just stunned to see their experience on the page.

It wasn't validation I was after.
It was *presence*.
A sense that Lily's memory had been *anchored* somewhere real.

At the final panel event — the last of the speaking engagements I agreed to — someone asked:

> "If you could say one thing to her now, what would it be?"

I didn't hesitate.

"Nothing."

"Nothing?"

"Yes.
Because she doesn't deserve the last word.
The girls do."

The next day, Georgia and I visited Lily's grave.

We didn't go often.
Not because we forgot —
but because Lily had always hated being seen in one place, tied to a single identity.

She liked fluidity. Movement.

Still, we brought wildflowers.
The kind she once pressed into the margins of her notebook pages.

Georgia laid the stems down gently.

"I wish she could see it," she whispered.

"She can," I said.

And I meant it.

We stayed until the light faded.

No grand speeches.
No declarations.

Just presence.

Silent. Whole. Alive.

And when we finally left,
we didn't look back.

Because we weren't running anymore.

We were walking forward.

Together.

The People Who Picked Up the Pieces

The Survivors Reclaim Their Names

Healing doesn't come all at once.
It comes in fragments.
A returned memory. A full breath. A sentence spoken out loud for the first time.

That's what we saw after Marianne vanished.

Not a flood of justice.

But a slow, steady gathering of women — and a few men — who had been rewritten.

They came from cities, from quiet villages, from hospital programmes and alternative therapy groups.

They came with fragments.

> "I think she made me believe it was my fault."
> "She told me to burn my journals — I did."
> "I was fifteen. I thought she was saving me."

They came with rage.
With grief.
With confusion.
And, eventually, with *names*.

Because Marianne's favourite trick was to make people forget who they were.

And now, one by one, they were reclaiming it.

Georgia's platform, *The Story You Were Told*, began to grow.

Not viral.

Not polished.

Just honest.

A submissions page. A survivors' circle.
A blog.
A directory of therapists who had been verified, by other survivors, as safe.

No certification programme.
Just something more powerful.

Trust.

One entry stood out. It was posted at 2:14 a.m. on a rainy Monday:

> *"My name is Zara. I used to go by 'Zed' because she told me my full name made me sound unreliable.
>
> She called me difficult. Said I was too attached to my story.

But that story?
It's mine now.

She doesn't get to keep it."*

It was signed:
Zara M. — Not a victim. Not a diagnosis. Just Me.

Georgia printed it.

Framed it.

Put it above her desk.

And that became our quiet mantra.

She doesn't get to keep it.

Meanwhile, I received emails from old colleagues.

Some apologised.

Some didn't.

But one — a former admin assistant who'd worked weekends at the original clinic — wrote this:

*I always knew something was off.
I just never knew what to say.

I'm sorry I didn't say it then.

But I'm saying it now.

Thank you for not staying silent.*

I didn't reply.

Not because I didn't care.

But because the reply wasn't for me to give.

It belonged to the girls.

The ones she tried to silence.

The ones we're still learning to hear.

The Women Who Stayed Silent Too Long

Not every survivor came forward.
Some never would.

And that's not failure.
That's *self-preservation*.

Because speaking is not the only way to survive.

Some women chose quiet.
Not because they were afraid —
but because they were *done* giving her space in their mouths.

Georgia once said,

> "There's bravery in silence when it's your own."
> "The problem was — hers was always made ours."

But a few did return.

Years after they left therapy.
After changing countries, names, entire lives.

They sent short notes. Unattached to email addresses.
Sometimes handwritten. Always unsigned.

One, in particular, stayed with me.

Written on torn notebook paper. Folded into thirds.

*She made me believe grief was a weakness.
So I buried it under performance.

But it leaked.
Into my relationships. My body. My skin.

I still don't trust therapists.
But I trust myself again.
And maybe that's enough.*

Another one simply said:

*You don't know me.
But she did.

Thank you for remembering what I couldn't
say at the time.*

Some women came in sideways.

A comment on a forum.
A paragraph in a memoir.
A character in a short story who bore too many
similarities.

And we never pushed.

Georgia was firm on that.

"This isn't about making everyone speak.
It's about making sure no one *has to lie*
again."

For every girl who posted publicly, ten more sat at home rereading the article, refreshing the site, waiting to feel safe.

We built for them.

Not a monument.

A mirror.

One that didn't distort.
One that didn't smile back with false care.
One that simply *reflected* what they'd been through and whispered,

"Yes. I see you. You're not making this up."

And quietly, power began to shift.

Not legally. Not even structurally.

But emotionally.

That was the piece Marianne had always underestimated.

Her control didn't rely on institutions.

It relied on *self-doubt*.

It relied on the belief that no one would ever validate the ache.

That no one would ever say,

"Yes. It happened.
And no — it wasn't your fault."

So we said it.

Over and over and over.

Until some of them began to say it for themselves.

The Silence That Turned Into Song

There was a moment — a quiet, unannounced one — when I realised we had crossed a threshold.

It wasn't dramatic.
It wasn't marked by headlines or inquiries or any external milestone.

It was marked by a voice.

One of the girls — Amara — had taken part in Marianne's group sessions nearly a decade earlier.
She'd been withdrawn, sharp-edged, untrusting.
Dismissed as "resistant to process" in her notes.

She messaged Georgia first.
Then me.

She said she was writing music again.

Not to heal.

To *remember*.

She sent a demo track — raw vocals, no production.

It was called **"Unscripted."**

And the chorus broke something open in me.

> *She told me how to tell my story
> In a voice that wasn't mine

But I kept a little ember
In the corner of my spine

Now I'm singing without shame
Not her rhythm, not her rhyme

Just me. Just truth. Just mine.*

We played it at the next survivors' gathering.

In a room above a community centre in East London, on a rainy Wednesday night.

Nothing formal.
Just chairs in a circle, tea gone cold, too many biscuits.

We sat and wept.

Not because it was sad.

But because it was *real*.

Because someone who had been made to feel like background noise
had become her own chorus.

That's how the song spread.

One woman learned the chords.

Another translated the lyrics into Spanish for a girl in Seville who had reached out.

Someone else added strings and uploaded it under a pseudonym.

No monetisation. No copyright.

Just a quiet anthem of reclamation.

It became a soundtrack to the healing.

A kind of protest, without the marching.

She told me how to tell my story…

But now, we were writing our own verses.

Georgia joked that we should record a compilation: *"The Songs She Tried to Silence."*

And for a second, I thought — maybe we should.

Because for so long, Marianne had made sure the only sound that filled those therapy rooms was her own voice.

But now, those rooms — the real and metaphorical ones — were *ours*.

And they were filled with music.

With truth.

With laughter.

With beginnings.

I still have the original recording.

It lives in a folder on my laptop titled *"Lily's Legacy."*

Because even though Amara never met her, the note still rang true.

> *Not her rhythm, not her rhyme.*
> *Just me. Just truth. Just mine.*

The New Language of Recovery

After everything, language became our soft revolution.

The same words Marianne had once wielded like scalpels
—

resistant, dramatic, dissociative, non-compliant —
we began to reclaim, soften, re-translate.

We didn't just talk about healing anymore.
We talked about *naming*.

Because once you name something — truthfully, fully — it
loses its power to corner you in the dark.

One of the survivors, a former poet turned therapist,
started a workshop called *"Retelling Without Permission."*

It filled within days.

Not just with women who had survived Marianne's version
of therapy, but with those who had survived systems.
Families.
Partners.
Schools.

Each of them had something in common:
They'd been taught their story was *inconvenient*.

And they were finally ready to rewrite.

The workshop didn't begin with writing.

It began with words.

Each participant had to choose five labels they had been given.

Then, five words they chose for themselves.

I remember mine clearly.

Given:

- Over-involved

- Unprofessional

- Fragile

- Untrustworthy

- Suspect

Claimed:

- Witness

- Whole

- Unlearning

- Necessary

- Survivor

The room filled with tears before anyone wrote a thing.

One woman — barely twenty — stood up and said:

> "She called me unpredictable.
> But maybe I was just still growing.
> And that terrified her."

Another whispered:

> "She said I was addicted to my sadness.
> But it was the only thing that still felt like mine."

Georgia stood last.

She didn't read her list.
Just held it in her hands and said:

> "She erased my sister.
> So I will name her again and again and again,
> until the world sees the shape she left behind."

And they did.

The world did.

Slowly.

Through new voices.
Through stories reclaimed.
Through labels rewritten.

Grief became wisdom.

Anger became firewood.

Silence became a pause — not a prison.

We built a glossary.

Not of psychological terms.

Of *truths*.

- **Resistant** = Protective.

- **Manipulative** = Desperate to be heard.

- **Non-compliant** = Setting boundaries.

- **Attention-seeking** = Asking to be loved.

We posted it online.

Not as a guide.
As a *gift*.

To anyone who'd ever been told they were "too much"
or "not enough"
or "in need of rewriting."

And in the margins of that glossary, we left one sentence bold:

> *Your voice is not a diagnosis.*
> *It's a return.*

The Return of the Unwritten

By the end of that year, the world had moved on.

New scandals filled headlines.
New names. New systems to question.
And Marianne — or Naomi, or Marie, or whatever name she would wear next — disappeared again into the quiet corners where people like her flourish best.

But the difference now?

We were watching.

And this time, we were *writing it down*.

The survivors' archive grew.
Quietly. Consistently.
Not just stories of harm, but of *rebuilding*.

A woman in her sixties wrote of starting therapy again, on her own terms.
A teenager who had once been told she was "too damaged to help" shared her first published poem.
A mother wrote that she finally believed her daughter, ten years too late — and was learning how to show up better now.

There were no monuments.

No national apology.

No plaque on the crumbling clinic wall.

But there was *presence*.

And that was more powerful.

The last thing I wrote in my journal that year wasn't for publication.
It wasn't for Georgia, or the survivors, or any article.

It was for Lily.

> *You weren't difficult.
> You weren't too much.
> You weren't a case to manage or a file to archive.
>
> You were a girl who asked to be seen.
> And I'm sorry I blinked.*

I keep her photo now.
Not the one from the clinic, but one Georgia gave me —
Lily at a beach, sleeves rolled up, wind-tangled hair and the kind of smile that doesn't ask permission.

She's not just a chapter anymore.

She's the reason the book exists.

In the end, *The Lie She Promised* wasn't about Marianne.

It was about the voices she tried to quiet.

The truths she failed to erase.

And the stories — plural — that rose like weeds through the cracks she left behind.

Uncontrollable.
Unedited.
And, finally, heard.

The Ghosts That Stayed Behind

The Things That Still Wake Me

Even after the noise faded, some things didn't leave.

Not guilt — I'd learned to live with that.
Not fear — that came and went like a tide.

What stayed were the *echoes*.

The half-sound of a voice I knew wasn't real.
The instinct to look over my shoulder in the queue at the post office.
The urge to flinch at emails that began with "Dr Whitaker…"

I'm not a doctor anymore.
But some ghosts don't care about qualifications.

I dream in transcripts.

It's ridiculous, and oddly specific.

Sometimes I'm in the room with Marianne again, but instead of speaking, we're reading from files.
Pages turn.
Ink smudges.
And then she looks at me and says:

"You wrote this, didn't you?"

I always wake up before I answer.

Other nights it's Lily.

She doesn't accuse me.

She just stands in the middle of a room and waits.

Not angry. Not hurt.

Just *there*.

I used to think it was guilt manifesting.

But Georgia told me something once — when we sat on the cliffs behind my house after the last inquiry session.

> "Maybe she stays because she wants to see what happens next.
>
> Maybe she trusts you to finish the story."

That changed things.

Not overnight.
But steadily.

I stopped fighting the ghosts.
Started listening instead.

Not all hauntings are curses.

Some are *reminders*.

That you lived.

That they lived.

That it mattered.

I still hear Marianne's voice sometimes — not as often, not as loud.

But when I do, it sounds different now.

Like an actress fumbling the same old script.

And I find myself whispering, without rage:

> "I don't believe you anymore."

That's the thing about ghosts.

They fade.

But only when you *name them*.

The Rooms That Still Remember

Some buildings forget.

They shed their memories with every paint job, every new owner, every layer of laminate flooring.

But others…

Others remember everything.

The clinic — what's left of it — is gone now. Demolished. Flattened. A block of identikit flats stands in its place, all light-grey render and glass balconies.

But every time I pass it, something in my chest tightens.

Not because I miss it.

Because it *still knows me.*

I walked past recently.

By accident — or maybe not.

Georgia was with me. We were on our way to a meeting about safeguarding reform, one she was invited to speak at. She carried a clipboard and an anger that looked more like purpose these days.

I stopped across the road.
She stopped too.

The building was new, but the shape of the land hadn't changed.

There was still that bend in the pavement. Still the wind funnel that caught your coat as you turned the corner.

I said, "It's strange. Nothing's left, but I can still feel her inside it."

Georgia nodded.

"Maybe it's not her anymore. Maybe it's you."

The rooms aren't physical anymore.

They exist in memory.

In stories passed between survivors.
In therapy notes annotated in hindsight.
In a song lyric, a transcript, a breath held too long.

There was a girl from one of the early retreats — a woman now, with a son and a life and a resilience you couldn't measure.

She wrote to me recently.

> *I sometimes find myself repeating her phrases when I'm tired or trying to calm myself down.*
> *It's like she built a house in my brain, and sometimes I don't even notice I've gone back inside it.*

But now, I'm redecorating.
Room by room.

That line gutted me.

And healed me.

At the same time.

I used to believe Marianne had built something permanent in all of us.
That her words would echo long after her name stopped being spoken.

But now I see it differently.

She didn't build us.

She *interrupted* us.

And we continued anyway.

The rooms may still hold her shape.

But we've turned them into something else.

Into pages.

Into art.

Into places we can finally walk through without flinching.

The Letters We Never Sent

There's a folder on my laptop called **Unsent**.

Inside it:
Forty-six letters.
All addressed to Marianne.

None of them sent.
All of them needed.

I started writing them when the inquiry first opened — not out of hope that she'd read them, but because some things have to leave the body, even if they land nowhere.

Letter #1 began politely.

> *Dear Marianne,*
> *I still don't know which part of you was real.*
>
> *Was it the woman who told me I had insight?*
> *Or the one who used my silence as permission?*

Letter #18 wasn't polite.

> *I hope you read your own notes someday.*
> *I hope you see the shape of what you made,*
> *and I hope it haunts you —*
> *not as punishment,*
> *but as truth.*

Letter #31 was about Lily.

She tried so hard to please you.
You praised her when she blamed herself.
And when she needed you to say, "It wasn't
your fault,"
you told her pain was a choice.

She didn't choose to die.
But she stopped choosing you.

Georgia wrote letters too.

Hers were shorter.

You made me question my sister's memory.
You made me feel embarrassed for believing
her.
I'll never forgive you for that.
But I'll never stop telling her story either.

None of us sent them.

And that's important.

Because the letters weren't for her.

They were for *us*.

To write without being edited.
To rage without being rationalised.
To say, "You hurt me,"
and not be told we were too sensitive.

Sometimes healing isn't a circle.
It's a spiral.

You pass by the same pain, but each time with more clarity.

Each letter brought me closer.

To the truth.

To myself.

To the part of me that still winced when I heard the word *therapist*.

Until eventually…

I stopped writing to her.

And started writing to the girls.

To Lily.

To Zara.

To Amara.

To myself.

>*You were never too much.*
>*You were just more than she could control.*

>*And now, you are free.*

The Weight of What Wasn't Said

For all that was spoken, printed, shouted, whispered —
there is still a heaviness in the things that never made it
out.

Not because they weren't important.

But because they were *too* important.

Too raw.
Too tangled.
Too afraid of being misunderstood — again.

There were things I never said at the inquiry.

Like the time I watched Lily leave Marianne's office,
red-eyed, gripping her own wrists like they were the only
thing tethering her to the earth.

Or the way Marianne once looked at me after a difficult
session and said:

> *"You have to decide if you're a witness…*
> *or just another unreliable narrator."*

At the time, I laughed.
Because I thought she meant it metaphorically.

Now I know it was a warning.

There were things the other girls didn't say either.

Because we're conditioned to measure our stories.

To second-guess:

> "Was it really that bad?"
> "Did I exaggerate?"
> "Maybe she was just trying to help."

The most dangerous trick she pulled wasn't deception.

It was **doubt**.

It lingers long after bruises fade.

It makes you apologise for pain someone else caused.

It makes you hesitate — even now — before saying:

> "What she did to me was real."

That's the silence I carry most.

Not the one I gave her.

But the one I gave myself.

The times I edited my own story because I feared it would inconvenience the world.

The times I answered,

> "I'm fine,"
> instead of
> "I'm still undoing what she did."

Georgia said once:

> "We keep looking for closure like it's a clean ending.
> But some stories only offer understanding.
> And even that comes in pieces."

So we collect the pieces.

The words unsaid.

The letters unwritten.

The shivers no one saw.

We hold them.

Name them.

Let them breathe.

Because silence isn't just what happened.

It's what we survived.

The Ghost That Finally Let Go

It happened on an ordinary morning.

Nothing significant in the sky.
No milestone to mark.
Just toast half-burned, sunlight through tired curtains, and the quiet murmur of the radio.

I was brushing my teeth when I realised something had changed.

I hadn't thought about her — Marianne — in days.

Not consciously.
Not in fear.
Not in preparation.

She hadn't narrated my movements.
Hadn't shadowed my decisions.
Hadn't whispered in the back of my mind that I was still, somehow, not finished with her.

It was like a fever breaking you never knew you had.

And I cried.

Not because I missed her.

Because I didn't.

Because I was finally *empty* of her.

The ghost hadn't left with the article, or the inquiry, or the book.

It left in the quiet.

In the ordinary.

In the space I finally made for *me*.

And I understood something then:

She was never going to apologise.

There would be no moment of justice that fixed everything.

But there could be **peace**.

And I had earned it.

I emailed Georgia later that day.

Subject line: *She's gone.*

No explanation needed.

She replied:

> *Told you she'd get bored once we stopped listening.*

The house feels different now.

Not just cleaner.
Lighter.

The mirror above the stairs doesn't scare me.
The notebook on my desk isn't guarded anymore.
The voice in my head sounds like *mine* again.

The ghost didn't leave with vengeance.
She left with irrelevance.

And that, in the end, was the deepest cut.

Because she wanted to be remembered.

Instead, she's *finished*.

The Ending She Never Expected

This Was Never Her Story

If Marianne were telling this story,
it would have ended differently.

She'd be the misunderstood visionary.
The woman ahead of her time.
The scapegoat for a system too afraid to face its own shadows.

There'd be elegant metaphors.
A closing quote about the burden of healers.
A final line like, *"Some truths are too raw to be told by anyone but the broken."*

She'd paint herself in grief.
In soft blame.
She'd weaponise vulnerability like only the dangerously charismatic can.

But here's the thing:

This was never her story.

The real story began the day Lily died.

Not because she was the first.
But because her silence echoed loud enough to crack the walls.

She became the fault line.
The tremor.

And everything that followed — Georgia, the dossier, the others who came forward —
all of it began with that moment.

With that girl.

With the question she left behind:

If I don't make it, will they tell it right?

So we did.

Not perfectly.
Not completely.

But truthfully.

With every page.
Every name reclaimed.
Every woman who wrote "Me too" and meant it deeper than the hashtag ever allowed.

Marianne didn't expect this ending.

She expected shame.
Retraction.
For us to collapse beneath the weight of our own complicity.

She thought we'd turn on each other.

Or on ourselves.

She underestimated what survivors do when they're believed.

What happens when doubt is replaced with solidarity.

She thought she was the narrator.

But she was just a chapter.

A necessary one.

A haunting one.

But not the last one.

Because here's what really happens,
when the lie breaks:

People listen.
People speak.
And the silence becomes a platform.

Not for her.

For **us**.

The Story She Couldn't Stop

When you spend long enough inside someone else's narrative,
you begin to forget how your own voice sounds.

That was her trick.

She didn't steal stories.

She replaced them.

Subtly.
Patiently.
With reassurances that felt like therapy —
but were really erasure.

And for a while, it worked.

Even after she vanished, there were traces.

I'd pause before speaking.
Filter my own memories for "usefulness."
Question whether my pain was *performative*.

Because she had planted that word in all of us.

"Performative."

As if grief were a play.
As if crying too long made you disingenuous.
As if healing could only happen in silence.

But the story didn't end when she left.

It *spilled.*

Freya's second article — the one she published after the inquiry closed — included a line I come back to often:

> *"There are people who help you rewrite your story.*
> *And there are people who hold the pen for too long."*

Marianne never gave the pen back.

So we had to take it.

Georgia once said:

> "What if survival is just getting loud again?"

And we did.

We wrote.
We sang.
We testified.
We whispered in coffee shops.
We called out phrases we used to swallow.

And the most radical thing?

We started making *joy* loud again too.

Because in the end, the story she couldn't stop wasn't about pain.

It was about what happens when truth survives revision.

It was about what happens when women remember the original draft of themselves.

The one before control.
Before containment.
Before the mirror only showed her reflection.

The final act of reclamation was this:

We no longer needed her name to name what happened.

The survivors didn't just survive her.

They *outlived her story*.

And built their own.

Becoming the Author Again

For the longest time, I thought healing meant erasure.

That to be well was to forget.
To forgive.
To let go so fully that the past no longer held shape.

But I was wrong.

Healing isn't forgetting.

Healing is *authorship*.

It's putting your name back on the page where someone else once wrote theirs.

In the months after the final report was published — the one that would sit in dusty government archives, read only by those with reason — I started writing letters again.

Not to Marianne.

To the girls.

To every woman who sat across from her and shrank.

To every one of us who translated pain into performance because we were told it was the price of being seen.

To the ones who didn't make it.

And the ones who are still reassembling the parts of themselves left behind.

The first letter was simple:

>*You're not a chapter she gets to keep.*
>*You're the author now.*

The second:

>*Your breakdown wasn't failure.*
>*It was resistance.*

The third:

>*You are not a diagnosis.*
>*You are not a cautionary tale.*
>*You are not what she told you you were.*
>
>*You are the evidence that her story ends here.*

Some letters I posted online.
Some I read aloud at support circles.
Some I kept just for me.

But each one stitched something back together.

A kind of narrative scar tissue.
Visible. Resilient.
Undeniably mine.

And that's what this book became.

Not an exposé.
Not a revenge piece.

A **return**.

To my voice.
To Lily's memory.
To every line of dialogue she never got to finish.

Because in the end, healing didn't come from destroying Marianne.

It came from *surviving her version* of us
and writing something new.

The Girls Who Rewrote the Ending

They don't call themselves survivors anymore.

Not all of them, anyway.

Some say *witnesses*.
Some say *rewriters*.
One girl, Ellie — whose voice used to vanish into her sleeves — now introduces herself in workshops as:

"A woman who wasn't erased."

There's something defiant in it.
Something soft, too.
Because survival wasn't the final chapter.
Reclamation was.

They started a collective.

Nothing formal. No hierarchy.
Just a network of women who'd been told too many times they were unreliable, dramatic, too sensitive, too quiet, too *something*.

The collective's tagline?

"We tell our own stories now."

They meet in borrowed rooms.
Back gardens.
Online calls with terrible Wi-Fi.

And still —
the storytelling is electric.

They read out letters they once hid in drawers.
They laugh at things that once made them shake.
They write their old therapist's names on slips of paper and burn them in tin buckets — not to curse, but to *release.*

One girl read a poem titled *Diagnosis: Human.*

Another taught herself embroidery and stitched the word *enough* onto old pillowcases.

One of the youngest there, barely eighteen, brought a shoebox of childhood diaries.
She read aloud the passages where she'd tried to be *good.*
To be the client Marianne would praise.

We cried.
We clapped.

Then we rewrote the entries with her.

In felt-tip pens and permanent ink.

These are not women who need saving.

They are the **storytellers now**.

Not victims.

Authors.

Georgia comes to every other meeting.

She sits in the back.

Sometimes she speaks.
Sometimes she just listens.

Always, she brings tea.

And one day, she brought something else:

A copy of Lily's birth certificate.
Framed.
With a note that said:

> *Her name is still here.*
> *And it always will be.*

That's what we're doing now.

Not surviving.
Not avenging.

Remembering.

Truthfully.
Loudly.
Without apology.

The Last Word Was Ours

There's no neat ending to this.
No final court ruling.
No televised reckoning.
No moment where Marianne stood and said, "I did this."

But we stopped needing her confession.

Because we had our own.

We confessed the truths we'd edited.
The pain we'd diluted.
The girls we'd once been — pliable, uncertain, desperate
to be believed —
and the women we are now.

Not saints.
Not broken.

Just *whole*,
because we wrote ourselves back into existence.

The last page of the archive Georgia built doesn't list
diagnoses.

It lists names.

First names.
Real names.
Chosen names.

Not for publication.
But for memory.

Zara.
Lily.
Amara.
Ella.
Frances.
Joy.
Georgia.
Me.

We are not footnotes.

We are the reason this story has *weight*.

There's a photograph taped to my desk now.

Taken at one of the collective's summer meetings.

A picnic blanket.
Mismatched mugs.
A daisy chain around someone's ankle.
Women mid-laugh, half-chewing, unapologetically alive.

In the corner, a little girl — one member's daughter — is painting everyone's hands with glitter glue.

She doesn't know what we've lived through.

But she knows we are safe.

And *that*, more than any inquiry or article,
is the ending we fought for.

This wasn't the story Marianne wanted told.

It's the story she *couldn't stop*.

And it ends here.

With *us*.

For the Ones Still Writing

If you are reading this and feel the tremor of recognition —

in the questions, the silences, the not-quite-anger lodged under your ribs —
this is for you.

Not as closure.
Not as healing.

As permission.

Permission to doubt what they told you.

To remember in fragments, not chronology.

To speak even if your voice trembles — especially then.

To rewrite what you were too afraid to write the first time.

To stop making yourself palatable for people who misused your trust.

To stop saying "it wasn't that bad" just because they didn't see bruises.

To understand that the absence of proof is not the absence of truth.

There are people who will try to reframe your story.

To tidy it.
To summarise it.
To own it.

There are institutions that will ask for evidence you no longer have.

And there are voices — including your own — that will whisper:

"Are you sure it happened that way?"

Let me answer for you:

Yes.

Yes, you are sure.

Even if the details shift.
Even if the dates blur.
Even if you only remember how it made you *feel*.

That is enough.

You are enough.

If no one believed you before —
believe this:

You are not alone.

Not now.
Not in this.
Not ever again.

And if you haven't found the words yet,
or if the words feel like they belong to someone else's
mouth —
start here:

> *It wasn't my fault.*
> *I'm allowed to be angry.*
> *I am still writing.*

This book is a grave for the lies.

And a garden for every voice they tried to bury.

Water it.

Speak into it.

Let it bloom.

— Isla March

Manufactured by Amazon.ca
Acheson, AB